## ABOUT THE BANK STREET READY-TO-READ SERIES

More than seventy-five years of educational research, innovative teaching, and quality publishing have earned The Bank Street College of Education its reputation as America's most trusted name in early childhood education.

Because no two children are exactly alike in their development, the Bank Street Ready-to-Read series is written on three levels to accommodate the individual stages of reading readiness of children ages three through eight.

○ *Level 1:* GETTING READY TO READ (Pre-K–Grade 1)
   Level 1 books are perfect for reading aloud with children who are getting ready to read or just starting to read words or phrases. These books feature large type, repetition, and simple sentences.

● *Level 2:* READING TOGETHER (Grades 1–3)
   These books have slightly smaller type and longer sentences. They are ideal for children beginning to read by themselves who may need help.

○ *Level 3:* I CAN READ IT MYSELF (Grades 2–3)
   These stories are just right for children who can read independently. They offer more complex and challenging stories and sentences.

All three levels of The Bank Street Ready-to-Read books make it easy to select the books most appropriate for your child's development and enable him or her to grow with the series step by step. The levels purposely overlap to reinforce skills and further encourage reading.

We feel that making reading fun is the single most important thing anyone can do to help children become good readers. We hope you will become part of Bank Street's long tradition of learning through sharing.

The Bank Street College of Education

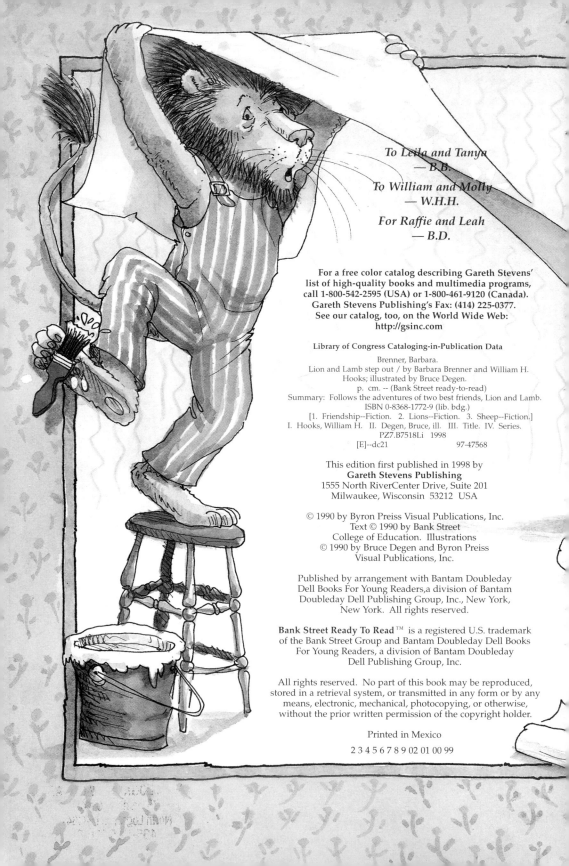

*To Leila and Tanya*
— B.B.

*To William and Molly*
— W.H.H.

*For Raffie and Leah*
— B.D.

For a free color catalog describing Gareth Stevens'
list of high-quality books and multimedia programs,
call 1-800-542-2595 (USA) or 1-800-461-9120 (Canada).
Gareth Stevens Publishing's Fax: (414) 225-0377.
See our catalog, too, on the World Wide Web:
http://gsinc.com

**Library of Congress Cataloging-in-Publication Data**

Brenner, Barbara.
Lion and Lamb step out / by Barbara Brenner and William H.
Hooks; illustrated by Bruce Degen.
p. cm. -- (Bank Street ready-to-read)
Summary: Follows the adventures of two best friends, Lion and Lamb.
ISBN 0-8368-1772-9 (lib. bdg.)
[1. Friendship--Fiction. 2. Lions--Fiction. 3. Sheep--Fiction.]
I. Hooks, William H. II. Degen, Bruce, ill. III. Title. IV. Series.
PZ7.B7518Li 1998
[E]--dc21 97-47568

This edition first published in 1998 by
**Gareth Stevens Publishing**
1555 North RiverCenter Drive, Suite 201
Milwaukee, Wisconsin 53212 USA

© 1990 by Byron Preiss Visual Publications, Inc.
Text © 1990 by Bank Street
College of Education. Illustrations
© 1990 by Bruce Degen and Byron Preiss
Visual Publications, Inc.

Published by arrangement with Bantam Doubleday
Dell Books For Young Readers, a division of Bantam
Doubleday Dell Publishing Group, Inc., New York,
New York. All rights reserved.

**Bank Street Ready To Read**™ is a registered U.S. trademark
of the Bank Street Group and Bantam Doubleday Dell Books
For Young Readers, a division of Bantam Doubleday
Dell Publishing Group, Inc.

Printed in Mexico

2 3 4 5 6 7 8 9 02 01 00 99

Bank Street Ready-to-Read™

# Lion and Lamb Step Out

by Barbara Brenner
and William H. Hooks
Illustrated by Bruce Degen

A Byron Preiss Book

Gareth Stevens Publishing
**MILWAUKEE**

# THE HIKE

Lion and Lamb were going on a hike.
"We'll need a snack," said Lion.
"I'll put some peanuts
in my backpack."
"And we'll need a map," said Lamb.
"A map always comes in handy
on a hike."

Lion went home to get ready.
In a little while he was back.
"All set," he said.
"Shall we go?" asked Lamb.
"Wait!" said Lion.
"Did you forget something?"
Lamb asked.

"Yes," said Lion.
"I forgot to tell you that
I must go first."
"Why is that?"
"Lions always go first," said Lion.
"Well—if you say so," said Lamb.
So Lion went first.
Off they marched,
singing a hiking song.

Soon they came to a place
where two roads met.
"Which way, pussycat?" Lamb called.
"This way," said Lion,
pointing with his paw.
"I guess you know," said Lamb.
"Lions always know," said Lion.
"That's why they go first."
"If you say so," said Lamb.

Next they came to a hill.

"Now we go over the hill," said Lion.

"That steep hill?" asked Lamb.

"Are you sure?"

"Lions are always sure,"
Lion snapped.

"If you say so," said Lamb.

They went over the hill.

On the other side of the hill,
there was a wide brook.
"Now what?" asked Lamb.
"Now we wade across the brook,"
said Lion.
"Maybe now we should look
at the map," said Lamb.

"Lions don't need maps,"
Lion growled.
"Never?"
"Never."
"If you say so," said Lamb.
They waded across the brook.

Lamb shook herself.

"Lion, I'm a little wet," she said.

"Lions never get wet," said Lion.

"Not even when they wade
across a brook?" asked Lamb.

"Not even when they wade
across a very wet brook," said Lion.

"And another thing," he roared,

"lions never get lost."

"If you say so," said Lamb.

Lion and Lamb hiked and hiked.
At last they came to
a field of flowers.
Lion said, "Let's have
our snack here."
"Good idea," said Lamb.
"Pass me a peanut, pussycat."
Lion reached into his backpack.
But all he found was a hole!

The peanuts were gone!
"Oh, no!" cried Lion.
"No snack. We'll starve!"
"Don't worry," said Lamb.
"When we get home, we'll have
a nice potpie."

There was a long pause.
Then Lion said, "Guess what."
"What?" asked Lamb.
"I don't know how to get home."
"You mean we're lost?" asked Lamb.
Lion nodded sadly.
"I was afraid of that," Lamb said.

"And the sun's going down,"
cried Lion.
"Things pounce when it's dark."
"Things *sleep* when it's dark,"
said Lamb.
"We're doomed," said Lion.
"Not a bit," said Lamb.
"We'll just look at the map."
Lion howled, "you see!
We *are* doomed!"
"Why?" asked Lamb.
"I didn't bring the map."

Lamb smiled sweetly.
"I didn't mean *that* map," she said.
And she pulled a map from
her backpack. "I meant *this* map.
You see," she said gently,
"lions may not need maps,
but lambs do."

Lamb unfolded her map.
"Hmmm," she said. "Hmmm."
She looked at it for a long time.
At last she said,
"All set. Shall we go?"
"You can go first," said Lion.
"If you say so," said Lamb.
And Lamb led the way home.

# UNCLE LEO

Lion and Lamb were on their way
to the circus.
"I can hardly wait to see Uncle Leo,"
said Lion.

"Is he the uncle who ran away?"
asked Lamb.
"Yes. He joined the circus.
Now he's a star."
"Think of that," said Lamb.
"I *am* thinking of it," said Lion.
"Uncle Leo must have lots of fun."
"Don't you have lots of fun?"
Lamb asked.
"My life is boring," said Lion.

"Don't you like to play
Chase-Your-Tail?" asked Lamb.
"Boring," said Lion.
"Don't you like to smell flowers?"
Lamb asked.
"Boring."
"Don't you like to hike?"
"Boring, boring, boring," said Lion.
"I may join the circus, too."
"Don't join yet, pussycat,"
said Lamb.
"First let's see the circus."

Lion and Lamb went into the tent.
"Look at all the animals," said Lion.
"Look at that man with the whip,"
said Lamb.

"The animals are running around the ring," said Lion. "That man is chasing them," said Lamb.

"Look! There's Uncle Leo,"
called Lion.
"The man is snapping his whip
at your uncle," said Lamb.
"He's making him roll over and over."
"That doesn't look like fun," Lion said.
"Why do you think Uncle Leo does it?"
"The man with the whip makes
him do it," said Lamb.

26

There was a loud sound of drums.
The man with the whip shouted,
"Ladies and gentlemen,
Leo the Lion will now jump
through a ring of fire."
Lion gulped. "Did he say fire?"
"That's what he said."
"Real fire?" asked Lion.
"*Hot* fire," said Lamb. "Some fun."
"Lions should never fool around
with fire," said Lion.

When the circus was over,
Lion and Lamb left the tent.
They went to look for Uncle Leo.
There were cages behind the tent.
Uncle Leo was in one of them.

"Uncle Leo!" Lion cried.
"What are you doing there?"
The big lion shook his head sadly.
"I didn't know about locked cages,
snapping whips, and rings of fire
when I ran away."

"But I thought the circus was fun,"
said Lion.

"Fun?" Uncle Leo said.

"Last week I burned my tail."

He put his head in his paws.

"So long, you two," said Uncle Leo.

"I need to rest before the next show."

Lion and Lamb tiptoed away.
"Where to, pussycat?" asked Lamb.
"Home," said Lion.
"You're not going to join the circus?"
"Never," said Lion.

"And you know what I'm going to do
when I get home?"
"What?" asked Lamb.
Lion smiled his pussycat smile.
"Something boring," he said.
"Something nice and boring."

# BEST FRIENDS

Lamb was on her way down the road.
"Where are you going?" asked Lion.
"Oh, I'm going to see a friend,"
said Lamb.

"Who?" asked Lion.
"Dog," answered Lamb.
"But dogs chase lambs."
Lamb picked a flower
and put it behind one ear.
"Dogs sometimes eat lambs,"
said Lion. "And they drool."
"Not this dog," said Lamb.
"He's my friend."

Lion plopped onto the ground.
He put his head between his paws.
His tail swished back and forth.
"Would you like to come with me?"
asked Lamb.
"Why would I want to do that?"
"All right, then," said Lamb.
"I'll see you later."

After Lamb walked on, Lion played
Chase-Your-Tail.
But it was no fun playing all alone.
He plopped onto the ground again.
"I guess you can't trust a lamb,"
he said to himself.

"Lamb said she was my friend.
Now she says Dog is her friend.
I hate dogs. They drool.
I should not have told Lamb
my secret.
I bet she'll tell Dog.

Now Dog and all the other animals
will know that I'm afraid to pounce.
I bet that Lamb is over there
right now, playing Chase-Your-Tail
and telling Dog *all* my secrets.
I might just go over to Dog's house.
I'm so mad, I think I really could
pounce on him!"

41

But Lion didn't go
over to Dog's house.
Instead, he wiped a tear
from his eye, curled up in a ball,
and went to sleep.

Something tickled Lion's ear.
He opened one eye.
There was Lamb holding a flower
and smiling.
"Hello, friend," she said.
"I'm not your friend," said Lion.
"Why not?"
"Dog is your friend,
so how could I be your friend?"
Lion asked.

"Don't we share secrets?" she asked.
"We did. But now Dog knows.
And it's not a secret anymore."
"What secret do you think
Dog knows?" asked Lamb.
"That I'm afraid to pounce,"
said Lion.
"I'd never tell that secret,"
cried Lamb.
"That's a secret between
best friends."

"You mean Dog doesn't know?"
asked Lion.
"Of course not," said Lamb.
"Then Dog is not your friend?"
"A lamb can have more than
one friend.
But you are my *best* friend."
"I am?" asked Lion.
"Now and forever," said Lamb.
"Now, friend, how about a game
of Chase-Your-Tail?"

Barbara Brenner is the author of more than thirty-five books for children, including *Wagon Wheels*, an ALA Notable Book. She writes frequently on subjects related to parenting and is co-author of *Choosing Books for Kids* and *Raising a Confident Child* in addition to being a Senior Editor for the Bank Street College Media Group. Ms. Brenner and her husband, illustrator Fred Brenner, have two sons. They live by a lake in Lords Valley, Pennsylvania.

William H. Hooks is the author of many books for children, including the highly acclaimed *Moss Gown*. He is also the Director of Publications at Bank Street College. As part of Bank Street's Media Group, he has been closely involved with such projects as the well-known Bank Street Readers and Discoveries: An Individualized Reading Program. Mr. Hooks lives with three cats in a Greenwich Village brownstone in New York City.

Bruce Degen has illustrated over twenty-five books for children, including the much-loved *Jessie Bear, What Will You Wear?, Jamberry, The Forgetful Bears Meet Mr. Memory,* and *The Magic School Bus at the Waterworks,* the illustrations for which were described as "hilarious" by the *New York Times Book Review.* Mr. Degen and his family live in New York City.